Brady Brady
and the Missed Hatrick

Written by Mary Shaw
Illustrated by Chuck Temple

PUBLISHED BY
BRADY BRADY INC.

Published in Canada in 2010 by

Brady Brady Inc.
P.O. Box 367
Waterloo, Ontario
Canada
N2J 4A4

Library and Archives Canada Cataloguing in Publication

Shaw, Mary, 1965 -
Brady Brady and the Missed Hatrick / written by Mary Shaw ; illustrated by Chuck Temple.

ISBN-13 978-1-897169-12-4

I. Temple, Chuck, 1962 - II. Title.

PS8587.H3473B7348 2010   jC813'.6   C2010-905399-0

Brady Brady loves hockey more than anything. At least that's what he thinks,
until his own carelessness almost costs him something more important.

Printed and bound in Canada

Keep adding to your Brady Brady book collection! Other titles include **Brady Brady and the:**

- **Great Rink**
- **Runaway Goalie**
- **Twirlin' Torpedo**
- **Singing Tree**
- **Super Skater**
- **Big Mistake**
- **Great Exchange**
- **Most Important Game**
- **MVP**
- **Puck on the Pond**
- **Cranky Kicker**
- **B Team**
- **Ballpark Bark**
- **Cleanup Hitters**

For Gayle and Steve,
Thanks for your friendship
Mary Shaw

The snowplow roared past Brady's house. "Hooray!" he shouted. "Our street is plowed. Come on, Hatrick."

Brady bundled up in his warm clothes and headed to the shed to get his hockey stick.

"Whoa there, Brady Brady," his mom said, taking the hockey stick out of Brady's hand and trading it for a shovel. "The driveway needs to be cleared before your dad gets home."

"Aw, Mom," Brady groaned. The plow had left a huge heap of snow at the end of the driveway.

Brady got to work. He was about halfway finished when he spotted Chester and Tes walking toward him, carrying a hockey net.

"Up for a game of shinny?" Tes asked.

Brady didn't give it a second thought. Abandoning the shovel for his hockey stick, he joined his friends.

Their fun was interrupted by the sound of tires spinning.
Brady's dad was stuck in the pile of snow at the end of the driveway.

"Oops! Gotta go,"
Brady told his friends and hurried off.

His dad did *not* look happy.

From then on, things went from bad to worse. His dad tripped over Brady's hockey bag and found the wet stinky equipment still inside. Brady had forgotten to air it out after yesterday's practice.

Brady's parents were upset that he was always rushing off to play instead of doing what he was supposed to be doing. They sent him to his room.

From his window, Brady could see the game of shinny still going on at the end of the street.

"Uh, Mom," Brady called.
"Should I take Hatrick for a walk before dinner?"

Brady's mom was thrilled that he was offering to walk the dog without being asked. Hatrick loved walks as much as Brady loved hockey.

When he reached the game, Brady tied Hatrick's leash to a lamppost and ran to join the game. Hatrick whined and yelped, but no one paid any attention.

Brady didn't feel the cold as he chased the tennis ball between both nets. But then it started to get dark and the game ended. Brady waved good-bye to his friends and ran home.

"Your dinner is getting cold," Brady's mom said, ruffling her son's hair. "At least Hatrick had a nice long walk." Brady's mouth dropped. His stomach felt like it had been punched.

"Say, where *is* Hatrick?" Brady's dad asked when he saw his son's face.

"I . . . I . . . tied him to a lamppost. I just played shinny for a couple of . . ." Brady's bottom lip started to quiver.

Brady's mom dragged him up the street in the dark. Under the streetlight, they found Hatrick's collar and leash – but no Hatrick. Brady fought back the tears as he and his mother walked the neighborhood, calling his dog over and over again.

Brady's dad and sister got into the car and drove around looking. There was no sign of Hatrick. Finally, they all had to give up and go home.

"Maybe he'll wander back on his own," Brady's mom said as she tucked Brady into bed. "I'll leave the shed door open for him, just in case."

Brady knew his mother was as worried as he was.

Brady stared at Hatrick's empty basket and listened to the winter wind howl. How could he have been so careless with his best buddy?

He tossed and turned all night.

Brady leapt out of bed in the morning to see if Hatrick had returned, but the look on his sister's face said it all.

Hatrick was still missing.

Brady felt too sick to eat breakfast. He couldn't look at his family. It was his fault they might never see their dog again.

His dad suggested going to the animal shelter to see if Hatrick had been brought in.

Brady rushed to go with him. It was better than doing nothing.

At the shelter, Brady ran from pen to pen, looking for his pal.

There, in the smallest cage, at the end of the last row, sat poor Hatrick. Brady tried to rattle the door open.

"Hold on, boy. I'll get you out of there," Brady whispered, sticking his fingers through the wire to touch his dog.

"Not so fast, son," said the attendant. "There's a shelter fee to get him back."

Brady's heart sank. He didn't have any money.

"I guess you'll be shoveling a lot of snow to earn that money," his father told him. "I'll *lend* it to you for now, but you'll have to repay me." He reached for his wallet. "I think that's the best way to teach you about responsibility."

He squeezed Brady's shoulder. "Besides, we can't leave our boy here, can we?"

"No, Dad," said Brady, handing the money over to the attendant. "And don't worry. I promise this will never happen again. One night without Hatrick was one night too many."

The man unlocked Hatrick's cage and winked at Brady.

"Take good care of that dog," he said. "He looks like a real good friend."

Hatrick's tail whipped back and forth faster than Brady's best slap shot. "I will," said Brady, not even stopping to wipe Hatrick's slurpy kisses from his face. "Let's go home, boy."

That day, Brady shoveled his own and four of his neighbor's driveways.

His friends came by to see if he wanted to play road hockey, but Brady told them he was too busy. He wasn't sure he had the strength to hold a hockey stick, anyway. Besides, he had a promise to keep.

In bed that night, Brady had just enough energy left to wrap his aching arms around Hatrick before he drifted off to dream about snowdrifts and shovels, cages and money, wagging tails and happy endings – and yes, hockey.